Dear Parents and Educators,

Welcome to Penguin Young Readers! As parents and educators, you
know that each child develops at his or her own pace—in terms of
speech, critical thinking, and, of course, reading. Penguin Young
Readers recognizes this fact. As a result, each Penguin Young Readers
book is assigned a traditional easy-to-read level (1–4) as well as a
Guided Reading Level (A–P). Both of these systems will help you choose
the right book for your child. Please refer to the back of each book
for specific leveling information. Penguin Young Readers features
esteemed authors and illustrators, stories about favorite characters,
fascinating nonfiction, and more!

Harry Takes a Bath

LEVEL **2**

GUIDED READING LEVEL **G**

This book is perfect for a **Progressing Reader** who:
- can figure out unknown words by using picture and context clues;
- can recognize beginning, middle, and ending sounds;
- can make and confirm predictions about what will happen in the text; and
- can distinguish between fiction and nonfiction.

Here are some **activities** you can do during and after reading this book:
- Word Repetition: Reread the story and count how many times you read
  the following words: clean, dry, quick, soap, splash, wash. Then, on a
  separate sheet of paper, write a new sentence for each word.
- Make Predictions: At the end of the story, Harry Hippo has cleaned up
  not only himself, but the bathroom, too. Discuss what you think Harry will
  do next. Will he make a mess of something else? If so, what?

Remember, sharing the love of reading with a child is the best gift
you can give!

—Bonnie Bader, EdM
　Penguin Young Readers program

*Penguin Young Readers are leveled by independent reviewers applying the standards developed by Irene Fountas
and Gay Su Pinnell in *Matching Books to Readers: Using Leveled Books in Guided Reading*, Heinemann, 1999.

Penguin Young Readers
Published by the Penguin Group
Penguin Group (USA) Inc., 375 Hudson Street, New York, New York 10014, USA
Penguin Group (Canada), 90 Eglinton Avenue East, Suite 700, Toronto, Ontario M4P 2Y3, Canada
(a division of Pearson Penguin Canada Inc.)
Penguin Books Ltd., 80 Strand, London WC2R 0RL, England
Penguin Group Ireland, 25 St. Stephen's Green, Dublin 2, Ireland (a division of Penguin Books Ltd.)
Penguin Group (Australia), 250 Camberwell Road, Camberwell, Victoria 3124, Australia
(a division of Pearson Australia Group Pty. Ltd.)
Penguin Books India Pvt. Ltd., 11 Community Centre, Panchsheel Park, New Delhi—110 017, India
Penguin Group (NZ), 67 Apollo Drive, Rosedale, Auckland 0632, New Zealand
(a division of Pearson New Zealand Ltd.)
Penguin Books (South Africa) (Pty.) Ltd., 24 Sturdee Avenue,
Rosebank, Johannesburg 2196, South Africa

Penguin Books Ltd., Registered Offices: 80 Strand, London WC2R 0RL, England

Text copyright © 1987 by Harriet Ziefert. Illustrations copyright © 1987 by Mavis Smith.
All rights reserved. First published in 1987 by Viking and Puffin Books, imprints of
Penguin Group (USA) Inc. Published in a Puffin Easy-to-Read edition in 1993.
Published in 2012 by Penguin Young Readers, an imprint of Penguin Group (USA) Inc.,
345 Hudson Street, New York, New York 10014. Manufactured in China.

The Library of Congress has cataloged the Puffin edition
under the following Control Number: 93002718

ISBN 978-0-14-036537-5   1 0 9 8 7 6 5

Harry Takes a Bath

by Harriet Ziefert
pictures by Mavis Smith

Penguin Young Readers
An Imprint of Penguin Group (USA) Inc.

Chapter 1
In the Tub

Time for your bath,

Harry Hippo.

Quick, quick,

up the stairs!

Towel,

soap,

warm water,

and washcloth . . .

everything is ready.

Jump right in!

SPLASH!

Splish, splash! Splish, splash!

Soap.

Soap up.

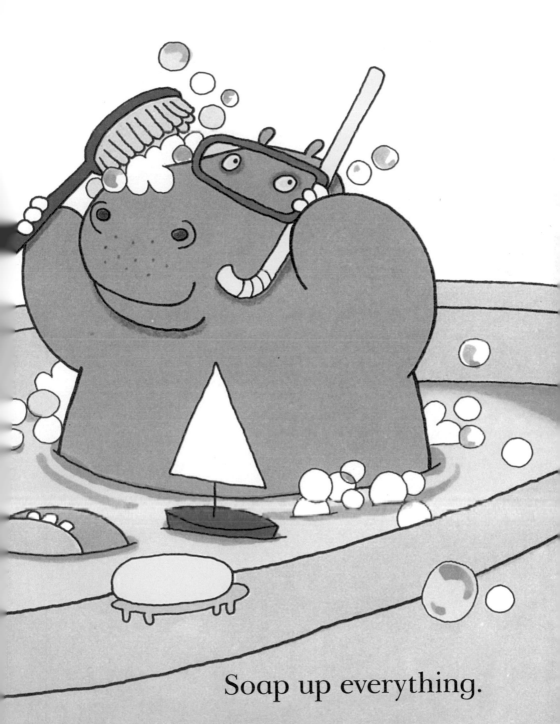

Soap up everything.

Wash.

Wash off.

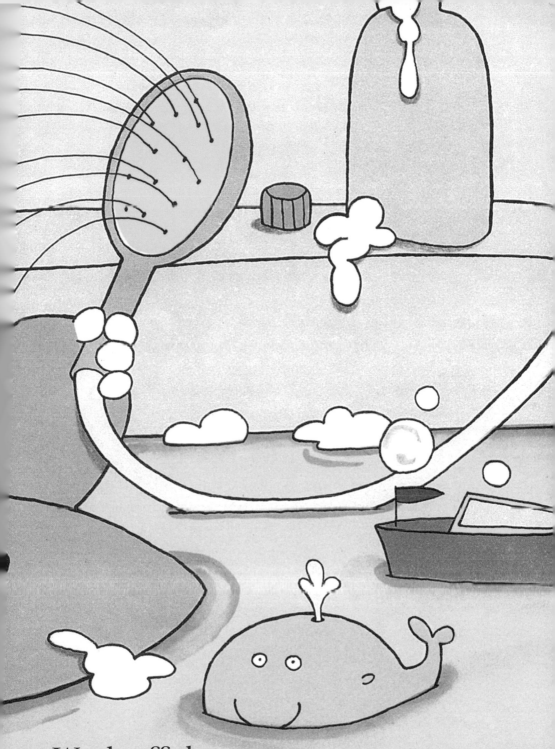

Wash off the soap.

Clean nose.

Clean ears.

Clean face.

Clean hands.

All clean!

Chapter 2
Out of the Tub

Quick, quick,

out of the tub!

Dry your ears.

Dry your face.

Dry your whole self.

All dry!

Now you can play some more!

The boat sails.

The whale swims.

Harry Hippo makes soap

pictures all over the bathroom!

23

Chapter 3
Clean Up

Clean hippo.

All clean!

Messy bathroom.

All messy!

Scrub the tub.

26

Scrub the wall.

Dry the whale.

Dry the boat.

Dry the water.

Hang up the washcloth.

Hang up the towel.

30

Everything is clean.

Good job,

Harry!